KT-384-104

VOICES

Blackburn, by those who know it

Edited by Sarah Dobbs

Copyright © all artists and authors, 2011

978-1-4709-1609-1

FOREWARD

I'm an outsider to Blackburn and first came to work here in 2010. What struck me was the sense of despondency in many of the people who lived and worked here. As a newcomer to the area, I could see a cutting-edge University Centre, a vibrant and diverse community with a fascinating history. There's innovation here, a rich tradition and an exciting potential future that we need to celebrate.

The *Voices* anthology was created to embrace all of the diversity and excitement that Blackburn has to offer. This collection comprises fiction, poetry and life-writing but definitions regardless, they are all stories about the town by people who have lived in, worked at and known it. Another aim of the anthology was to allow all types of writers to work together and to show that writing has a place in everyone's life. You don't have to consider yourself a writer to be able to write. You don't need an MA in Creative Writing or to be a published novelist to see the positive impact of writing on your life. *You don't need permission*. We can all write our stories and we all have something important to say, whether that's our memories of growing up to pass on to our families, a best-selling novel or prize-winning poem, or observations for our own personal notebooks.

To that end, this collection will tell you all sorts of stories. It will take you from real-life reminiscences of growing up, to poetry describing the beautiful sites and memories - some tough and gritty - that Blackburn has given our writers, to current experiences of what life is like now. *Voices* boasts some already well-known writers such as Tony O'Neill, Andrea Ashworth and Sarah Hilary. It also includes writers who have never written before and are discovering the importance of writing, from ten year old Lotte Gracie Neils' enchanting *Blackburn Library*, to Pauline Jackson's evocative accounts of *Slippy Baths* and *Saturday Nights*. Writing helps us see, it helps us to notice and explore the details. What has become apparent from the work submitted, is the acknowledgement that the town has its faults and that there are certainly many difficulties to overcome. The overwhelming feeling that emerges from these stories, despite some that acknowledge and explore the harsh reality of the place, is one of pride. I feel respect and compassion for those who have shared their stories here. We hope you'll enjoy the anthology, and that you'll appreciate the details our writers have noticed.

Have your own say on *Voices* by leaving your thoughts and feedback on our Wordpress site: http://blackburnvoices.wordpress.com. As a final treat, you can hear audio recordings from Sarah Hilary, AJ Ashworth, John Hindle and Mark Ellis at http://www.youraudiostories.tumblr.com.

Dr Sarah Dobbs

Lecturer in English and Creative Writing, UCBC

CONTENTS

ACKNOWLEDGEMENTS

Voices could not have become a reality without the following people. We would like to thank Kelly Milaszewicz for her enthusiasm and for providing us with such fitting and amazing photographs, including the striking cover image. To Jim Valentine for his wonderful interpretation of Tony O'Neill's poem. To BBC Radio Lancashire for allowing us to broadcast our intentions for the project and to Blackburn library for helping us to put out our initial submissions call. Finally, our heartfelt appreciation goes to all the writers who submitted and to all of those in the anthology. We appreciate you sharing your words and letting your voices be heard.

AFTER A LONG ILLNESS, QUIETLY AT HOME

Sarah Hilary

First, I want to show you his room.

Lemon walls, a bit greasy just there above the bed. And yes. Should've washed his hair more often. He hated me to touch him though, especially towards the end: 'You're not my ruddy wife!'

Foreign embassy. Listen to them talk. All about his honourable service. Surely, I think, someone else knew the truth. How am I all alone? Formica, the bedside cabinet. Look at the cup rings, Vaseline and whatnot, a rare old mess.

A litter of tissues. Search them for lipstick insignia? Haven't the heart now, not now. Funny how the light in here makes everything flatter than it actually is. Linoleum floor; I wanted Axminster but he wouldn't budge.

'Axminster? Soon you'll have us with chintz bloody curtains.'

How about a rug, I said, and of course he made a comment about my hair.

For a while I thought of leaving him. Longed to, in fact. Asked at work about relocating. Sunnier climes?

'Ha ha! Bugger off then.' Ferocious sod had his pride.

Look.

At the shape of his head in the pillows. Still warm. Half a glass of water with his teeth inside. French letter. Library book. Andrew's Liver Salts. Spectacles, horn-rimmed. Handkerchief, spotty.

For what it's worth, I loved him. Lonely sort of love. Anyone asks, I wouldn't recommend it. See what it's done to me. Hitting the ditch from the pillows where his head lay, opening the windows to air a room where I was never welcome, not even when I brought breakfast and the post, not once in all these years, I should say *those* years, not once anyway and never when I brought the post.

'Flaming bills!'

Language, I'd say.

'And you can sod off!'

'Shall I turn back the bed?'

He'd look at me then, all sunken chest and self-reproach, and I'd pat his hand and pour the tea and two cups later he'd be fine.

THE COLOURS OF BLACKBURN

Maria Ismail

Rows of grey slated rooftops

under the dull, damp sky.

Domes of green and gold

Arabian nights,

lost in the moors

People bustling

Vibrant reds and yellow

illuminating dark shop windows.

Hard exteriors of stony terraces

A town buzzing with culture

on the brink of change.

Mix of East and West,

infusions of flavour

Spice warms the air.

The ringing of Cathedral bells.

The 'Adhan' echoing in the streets,

all have come out to play

They play and sing and dance,

begging not to be torn apart

If one was there and not the other

this place would be incomplete

But to me these colourful streets are home

The start of a rainbow after a storm.

"CHARACTERS OF OUR DISTRICT"

In the 50s and 60s our family lived up Grimshaw Park, street after street of terraced two up two down houses. We were very lucky to have a close knit community, people who lived, laughed and sometimes cried together. Everyone knew each other and we all knew the Characters of the district. These were the people who would entertain us all in one way or another just by being themselves, without knowing they were funny or amusing to others. One of these people was our milkman, Billy. He would come around every morning with his horse Bob, pulling the cartful of milk. He was a farmer's lad in his late 30s, ruddy complexion, one or two front teeth missing, with a flat cap on the side of his head, an overcoat three sizes too big for him and large wellingtons on his feet. Whatever the weather the milk would be on the doorstep before 10am. On Saturday mornings Billy had to deliver the milk, and he also collected his weekly money from his customers.

Bob seemed to know which house would feed him an apple or potato, as he would mount the pavement and put his head up to the front doors until we kids would open the door to pat his head. Billy would shout, 'Bob, come on, I ain't got all day,' as he was further down the street. Everyone knew why Billy would be in a hurry to finish his round. It was the only time Billy had free in his working week...Saturday afternoon, and he made the most of it. Bob would have his feedbag around his head, stood outside the 'Thowt it' pub on Grimshaw Park at about 1-30pm, Billy would have his pint glass in his hand inside the 'Thowt it' pub.

The pubs closed at 3pm in those days. Billy would climb onto his empty milk car to be pulled up Haslingden Road by Bob his faithful friend. Billy would be singing at the top of his voice, the more the neighbours waved to him, the louder he would sing. There were many of these characters. These neighbourhoods were not made up of bricks and mortar, but the people who lived there, who enjoyed living there, who were happy and content there, even though it was very old...but it wasn't to last. The authorities said the district was too old and had to be demolished to make way for modernisation. We all disagreed, young and old folk...we lost, they won. They flattened it all. We went to watch the giant crane with the swinging giant ball smashing into our houses. We stood and cried.

Pauline Jackson

UNTIL MORNING

Mark Ellis

Wendy's photo is on TV again. I sit there staring at it for a while. In reality she looks older - more tired, more empty. She's in the bath singing a song that I don't know. I go in, put the toilet seat down and sit there watching her. She smiles at me and I smile back. 'You alright?' I say.

She nods and then carries on playing with the flannel. Drawing it up and down her arms. Up and down her legs.

'Can we get nuggets for lunch?' she says.

'We had them last night.'

She shrugs.

'Have something different.'

'I like nuggets. The burger buns are always stale.'

'Hot dogs?'

'Same.'

'Nuggets don't need bread.'

'What about a chicken burger? Without bread.'

'Is there candyfloss?'

'I don't know.'

The phone rings. I go over and pick it up.

'Peter - She's on TV again. Every channel.'

I pick up the remote. Switch between channels. She's everywhere. I shrug to myself. 'It says they've got no leads.'

'They always say that.'

'It'll be ok.'

'You've fucking done it this time.'

'Nobody seems to be accusing *them* of neglect,' I say. 'You don't leave kids on their own. Everyone knows that. It's fucking neglectful.'

'Well, what you gonna do?'

'I don't know.'

Neverland is all skeletons. Broken lights. Peeling merry-go horses. We walk along Main Street, hands in pockets. The oil in the fryers makes refried doughnuts taste like bad fish. With meat it's ok. When they went, they left the freezers stocked. The oil takes a while to heat up so we have a go on the ghost train. Her in the carriage and me as the skeleton that breathes down her neck. Mostly she screams, today she cries for her mother. Afterwards I give in. We sit and eat the nuggets on a wall.

'What do you want to do today?'

She shrugs. 'Maybe just watch some TV?'

'We've got this whole place to ourselves.'

'Yeah.'

'Every ride.'

'I know.' She scrapes her foot along the floor.

I look at her. 'Is there a problem?'

She shakes her head.

'Do you want to go back?'

She shrugs.

'When there's all this?'

She half-smiles.

I stand up. 'Come on – I'll crank up the candy floss machine. That'll cheer you up.'

We walk over to the kiosk; I go inside and put on an apron. 'Remember when the vending machine ran out of tampons and we had to…'

'Don't.'

'I just…'

'Don't.'

'It was funny at the time.'

She looks at me. 'Just make the fucking candyfloss.'

'Bag or stick?'

'Does it matter?'

'It suffocates in a bag. You know that.'

'Well there's your answer then.'

I dip the stick in. Swirl it around. 'I don't know what's wrong with you.' I say.

'I want to go back.'

'I asked you that before.'

'Well I mean it.'

I hand her the candyfloss. 'What're you going to do?'

She shrugs.

'Well then...' I watch her eat the candyfloss. Afterwards she drops the stick on the floor and walks off. I clean down and shut the kiosk.

She's sitting in a bumper car. She's got her feet up on the front and she's smoking a cigarette. 'Sorry,' I say. She exhales. 'I didn't know you...When did you start smoking?'

'There's lots you don't know about me.'

'I know.'

She looks at me.

'You really want to go?'

'Yes.'

I sigh. 'After all this time? After everything?'

'It wasn't so much.'

I stand there looking at her.

She takes a drag on her cigarette and exhales.

'Do you remember the way?' I say. 'Second on the right and...'

'I know.'

I watch her go from the front seat of the kids' caterpillar ride. Scrunched in. The wind picks dust up in circles. The giant swans drift on the lake.

PISS TOWN

Tony O'Neill

going back

through institutional corridors

and overgrown secret paths

cutting across the back of the hospital

surgery scars on desolate hills

up the winding stone staircase

to an industrial ground-zero

of abandoned refrigerators

and dripping chimneys spewing

thick, grey chemical smoke

to the blackened wall

where I wrote the inscription

'Joy Division' in silver paint

sometime around 1992

when I close my eyes

the images play out

against the lids

a travelogue of childhood flashes:
piss town

from a secluded path where
an acne scarred girl charged one cigarette
for a hand-job and a glimpse of tit
to the crumbling, faux-Victorian pub
were I was served my first beer

the old, beaten-up whores
of Clayton Street lurking in the shadows
of the lumber yards and the gas works
waiting for trade to stumble drunkenly
from the twinkling lights of the pubs and clubs

the frozen image of a sad-eyed young girl
staring out window of a terraced house
and then stolen away in a flutter of net curtains
and a girl I once knew, half dead now,

crushed with poverty and port wine
two incubator babies and her insides
dumped into hospital bins before she turned thirty:
piss town.

I served my time
in dusty world war two bedrooms
you wrote your name in childlike letters
on a box of forgotten papers in a stifling attic

I severed my ties:

bled from my hands, my mouth, my pen
all of the others still locked behind
a sturdy steel door of drunken recollection
preserved in amber
hand frozen over a glass of bitter

forever wired on pink amphetamines

brutalized by the intervening years
some killed by work, some by knives,
women, and others by the steady
passage of time:
piss town

on the news
the US secretary of state
waving from the town hall steps
with the local MP (who lives in Whitehall)
both smiling stiffly beneath
the Sunday skies
how fitting – Basra, Gaza
and now here

while in The Swan those driven insane
by the brutal drudgery of it all
drink cider and whiskey to forget
to speed up time's monotonous progression

desperate to skip ahead

to the final act

a misty churchyard

a handful of mourners

it was a lovely service

just lovely:

piss town

but sometimes, alone

underneath the crumbling architecture

of Queen's Park hospital

looking down from my spot on the wall

at the empty bottles of Zeppelin and White Lightening

discarded bras and dosser's blankets

I'd close my eyes and listen

to the Imam's call to prayer

floating up from Audley Range

a welcome interloper from some inaccessible continent

the feel of the light, July wind

on my face, and I concede

there is something special here

hidden away from prying eyes

something private, unsayable,

neither from the council estates of Higher Croft

nor the abandoned terraces of Shakeshaft Street

something that appears at dusk

during stolen moments of peace like this

before it is inevitably carried away

from me again:

piss town

COTTON TOWN PROJECT

YOUTH ACTION

Youth Action gave me a chance to see and learn about Blackburn's historical background and also to talk to people who actually worked in the mills. The people who worked in the mills had experiences of Blackburn that were much different to mine. This helped me understand what Blackburn was really like. One of the cotton mill workers was from India and they came to England in 1966, where he was working at the age of 21 in a cotton factory. He told me about what he first saw when he got off the train; that the town-centre had really dark, soot covered buildings. These buildings were really tall compared to his small house back in India. He then told me what Blackburn College was like back then. He described the college as being quite small and really old, not like the college today. In the college class, there were only 11 students.

He then went on to talk about the bed and breakfast that he lived in when he first came to Blackburn. He said it was a small place with just a few residents staying. He was the only 'south Asian' in the bed and breakfast. This was not really a problem but the only thing he could eat was fish and chips. This was a really popular dish. In fact, he had it every night because the kitchen staff did not know how to cook curry or any other Indian cuisine. The mill worker told us that there were no takeaways like today, only fish and chip shops. He commented on the shops closing so early he could not even consider going to the shop after 5pm.

When he started working in the mill he was on £6.30 a week. I couldn't believe what he'd said so I had to ask him again. I thought, how could you live off just £6.30 but he said that it was quite manageable. After a couple of months working in the mill he got promoted and his salary went up to £13.00 a week. After a few more months he got promoted again and his salary went up to £18.00. He then decided to move out of the bed and breakfast and he wanted to rent out a small flat near town. He remembers looking at the flat and it was pretty decent. He only had to pay £3.00 per week to the landlord.

He said there were no differences between people back in the 1960's. Everyone wore similar clothes and the fashions were all similar. Asians were invited to everything from christening to funerals. They were accepted and respected. The cotton mill worker also told me that every English person he ever met was respectful to him and his religion and they even knew about the Muslim religion. 'No one would ever ignore us,' he said. 'They would always stop to say hello and have a conversation with us.'

There were secret relationships with coloured people and English people. He thought that this was because of the different religions and also because of the different cultural backgrounds that people came from and respected. He remembered talking to a girl when he was in college and they went out for a while, but they had to keep their relationship secret. The girl always said that if her dad found out they would not be too happy. But he didn't understand what the problem was really. But after five months of going out with this girl he wanted to marry her, so he had to ask her dad for their approval and he actually said yes.

The mills were really hard to work in and they were in a really bad condition. The mill worker remembers those days like it was yesterday. He said there was no canteen in the mill, you had to bring your own pack lunch or do without. There were no facilities for tea or coffee so you just had to drink water and that was quite a mercy. He also commented on the amount of dust that was in the mill and they didn't even provide a mask to cover your face. These days, the mill would have been closed down by health and safety but there was nothing like that then. The worker also remembered that the mills were really loud and you could not hear anything at all. He said that you had to learn how to lip read to communicate to people. He thought that this was a really hard thing to do but eventually he picked it up.

He remembers going to Clitheroe for a day out to go and look at the castle and take in some fresh air. After being in the town centre for 30 minutes or so lots of people started following him. He couldn't understand at first. But after a while a small boy came up to him, asking if he could stay there for a minute while he got his friend to look at him. He started to understand why people were following him. They had never seen an Indian man walking the streets if Clitheroe before, and they were absolutely amazed at him being there.

The worker also remembers going to Blackpool for the weekend, and this cost £2.00 for the bus there and back. Blackpool was a really popular holiday destination for people to go to, because it was rather cheap but mostly because there were no such concept of holidays abroad at that time. He remembers Blackpool being like today but a little smaller, and you could get a stick of rock for only ½ p or candy floss on a stick for only 1p.

I think from what he has said Blackburn has changed a considerable amount. This is mostly because there are not that many cotton mills that are still standing in Blackburn, never mind working anymore. Most of the buildings in

Blackburn have changed or even been knocked down, and there has been an increase in the population. With the changed landscape the people's attitudes and values seem to have changed. We can't go back in time, but we can learn a lot from the past.

INDUSTRIAL ANTHEM

Gaye Gerrard

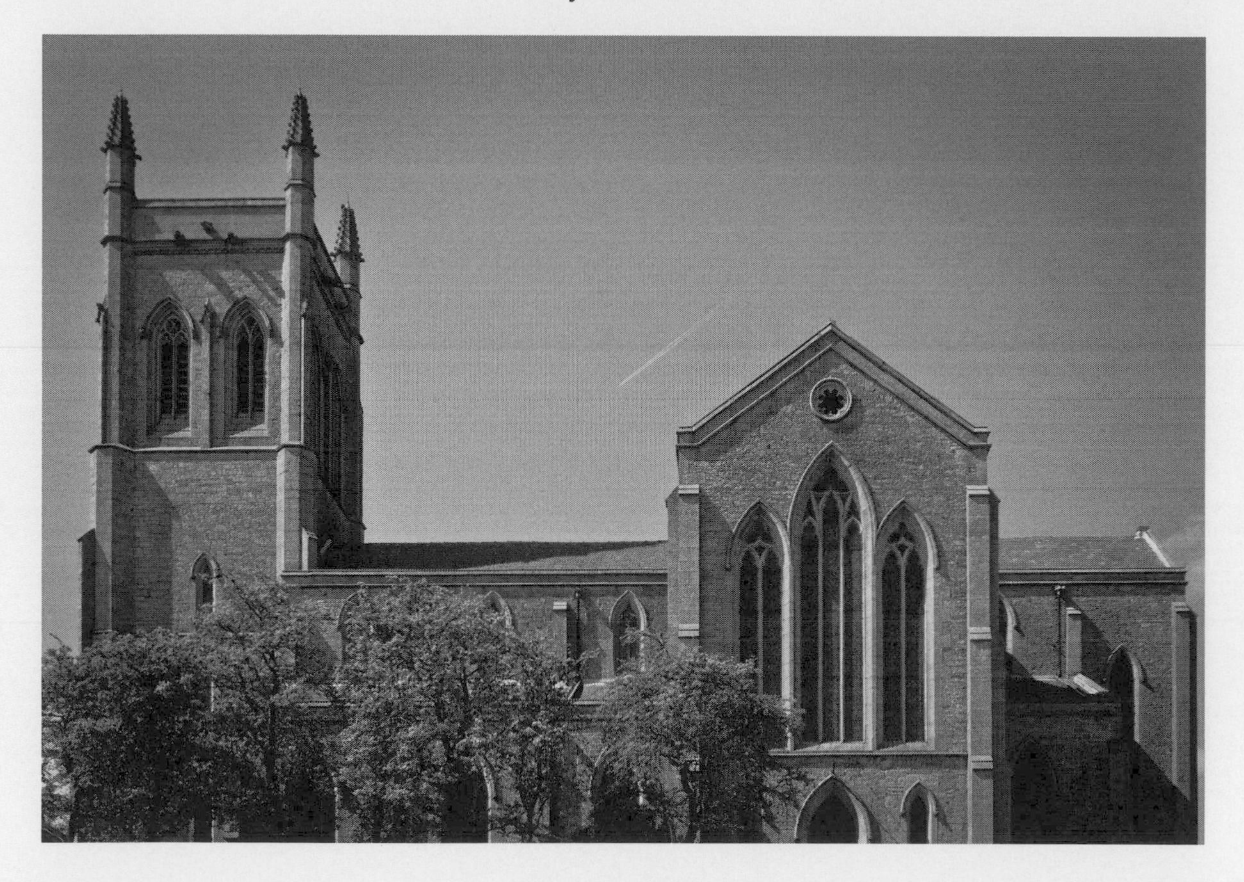

Cathedral sounds

Resound around me,

Sonorous and profound,

Blurring and merging

The present with the past.

I gaze through the haze,

Through the stifling heat

Hear the percussive beat

Of strap flap and ratchet tap

And asthmatic sighs.

With the hiss and the sneeze

Of the gradual release of steam

Six tons of fly- wheel slowly stirs,

Gathers momentum,

Til the boom and thrum

Become the bass note's beat

To the rhythm of life

In the industrial heart,

Become songs,

Exultant!

Triumphant!

The anthem of creation

Fills the mills of Cottonopolis!

And so it goes on,

The thump and the drone

Of the industrial machine

Creating abundance,

Men of substance,

Continuing to provide

Essential life blood.

To the textile trade;

Til, finally, it fades,

With a terminal moan,

A judder and a shudder.

A gasp and a long sigh

Still the mills of Cottonopolis

"SLIPPER BATHS"

It was always a treat when as a little girl, my mother would take me to the Freckleton Street Baths, about 20 minutes walk, or a couple of bus stops away from our house at that time. We didn't go swimming; we went to the Slipper Baths. I would carry the pump bag with towels bath salts, sometimes little coloured balls which made a bubble bath when placed under the taps, the hair brush and talc. The talc, bubble balls and perfumed bath salts had been Christmas or birthday presents to my mum. As I was only small, my mother's bath was enough for us both. I remember the big room was partitioned off into separate bathrooms. These deep white baths had wood surrounds with ledge I would sit on until the water cooled down enough for my liking. My mum would be in the steamy, bubbly water and I would stand at the opposite end until she told me to 'sit down or you'll slip and hurt yourself'.

Eventually, I would lower myself into lovely perfumed hot water which covered my shoulders. Once in, my mum had trouble getting me out, so she would dress and do her hair, then lift me out and dress me. My hair was long and curly. I didn't like it to be brushed when dry, but when it was wet all hell let loose, so my mum would quieten my howls with a promise of a penny loaf on our way home. These were miniature loaves baked at the confectioners on Canterbury Street, just round the corner from the baths. We kids loved them, they tasted nice and they were a novelty to us. I would tell my grandma and granddad we'd been to the ***slippy baths****. When they asked me what I meant I would* *explain to them, 'Cos, if you don't sit down when you get in, you'll slip under the water'. For years afterwards, Frecky Baths was known as Slippy baths in our house.*

Pauline Jackson

THE COMMUNITY (Dig In)

Ismail Karolia

That winter was particularly cold. The snow fell hard and settled quickly, rising from the ground like a ball pool being filled with cotton wool. The only thing missing was reindeer and a couple of huskies and this little Blackburn estate would have looked just like a scene from Alaska.

The bitter cold kept everybody inside, radiators left on high. Imran didn't want to go out, but knew he had to. His heels were already catching the back of his new snow boots. The thought of painful blisters was not the only thing putting him off. The biting cold against his skin and the lack of company made him question why he was going out at all. Still, it had to be done. He was confident in his new boots though; the sales girl had suggested them for the winter and the thick rubber grip seemed like it could stand up to the slippery ice. Until he fell on the drive. And then again, while opening the garage door. It was going to be a long morning.

Why he had insisted on buying expensive leather driving gloves, he would never know. As he dug the snow from the road, the friction from the spade and the leather would add some accompanying blisters to those on his feet. He'd been working for an hour, and the drive seemed pretty much as dangerous as when he started, if not more so. Still, he had created a wall of snow in the corner of the garden; no doubt some kids would appreciate the opportunity to destroy that masterpiece. He could see Psycho Sykes peering from her window, her curtain slightly edged back to reveal her face. Imran tried a half-hearted wave, just to see what reaction he would get. He could make out a stern glare. It would have to do.

He spread some rock salt on the drive. Now to start on the road. There was a tap on the glass behind him. His wife, Aliyah, beckoned him back inside. Imran blew her a kiss, and carried on scooping the snow from the ground. His aim was to get as much of the road clear as possible. Aliyah was nearly due and the roads would make it difficult to get to the hospital. Even worse, with how bad it was, the car might not even make it there. If only he could clear all the snow to the main road, but he was nowhere near.

Tony came down his path to open his boot. Imran saw him rummaging around. Tony kept one hand on his car as he edged around to talk to Imran.

'Ay up lad, you're hard at work aren't you?'

Imran smiled. Tony was a gent, always friendly. They hardly talked apart from in passing, but that was more than he talked to other neighbours.

'Is your missus alright?'

'She's ok Tony, due anytime now. That's why I'm out here, in case we need to get out.'

'How far are you expecting to clear?' One eyebrow was slightly raised. He obviously had a far more realistic view on the task Imran had set himself.

'To be honest I was hoping to get to the main road.'

Tony's hearty laugh made Imran feel sheepish.

'Sorry mate, but that's a real laugh. You're going to need some help. I'll just get my spade from the back garden and give you a hand.' Tony edged back along his car.

Had Imran heard right? Was it a joke? 'Tony! Don't worry about it, man. Honestly, it's ok.'

'It's ok, mate. I won't be much help at my age but wouldn't feel good leaving you out here on your own,' he said, trying to traverse his pathway.

He soon came back and, despite Imran's pleas, started shoveling snow and ice from the roads. As he and Imran were speaking, Imran realized this was probably the most they had ever said to each other, and although he felt awful having brought Tony out on a day like this, he was glad for the company.

Mr. Mahmood's deep, Pakistani accent interrupted them. 'What you boys doing, you crazy? It's freezing!'

Imran looked over at Mr. Mahmood's; he was peering out of his window. Imran half wished Tony wouldn't reply, but there was no stopping him.

'Hey, his wife's due soon and they're going to need a way out. Might as well come and help.'

Mr. Mahmood cringed. 'My back, you see, Tony. I just can't do these things anymore.' He closed the window, but returned moments later. 'I've told my boys to come and help. This job for young men. They're coming now, I tell them.' There was pride in his voice.

Salim and Ali came out, sharing neither the smile nor pride of their father.

'Hey,' they said, and started shoveling.

Soon enough the four of them were making progress. The two young men had their earphones in, barely saying a word. Tony and Imran talked about family and the experiences ahead for the happy couple. As they crept down the street other people noticed what was happening. The Williams' brought their 10 and 12 year old out, along with little spades.

'We've been looking for something to keep the kids busy,' Mrs. Williams said.

Jack and his grown-up daughter, Yvonne, joined in too. The elderly Mrs. Jones made a flask of tea and handed out cups.

'Come on you lazy beggars, no time for brews!' Yvonne called, and Salim dutifully listened. His headphones were in his pocket now.

The street was buzzing with activity, most people helping to clear the roads and paths, others enjoying the weather and spirit. Even Psycho Sykes' path got cleared.

Imran looked around, amazed. 'What just happened?' he murmured.

Children who barely spoke to each other were wrapped up making snowmen together. The men and women of the community were coming together, laughing and helping each other. It felt surreal. Imran was suddenly self conscious. Were they doing all this for him?

A hand gently clutched his shoulder. Behind him stood a thin man, wearing a shell suit jacket over a stripy shirt. He had dark skin and a pleasant smile.

'Hello sir, I saw you all working. I can help but I haven't got a spade.'

His thick, African accent showed he probably wasn't used to this weather, but he stood, hand stuck on Imran's shoulder, waiting for instructions.

Yvonne stepped in. 'Ok mate, you take this one, I'll get another.' She handed the man her shovel and he smiled, with a thank you and a nod of the head.

Tony asked the man his name; no one had seen him before. Although the community wasn't usually this vibrant, people still knew everyone's name. But Alexan, as was his name, was unknown. He had a calm demeanor, even as he awkwardly navigated the icy ground. He struggled at first to make an impact on the ice and was noticeably pleased when he started breaking through. Imran and Tony found out Alexan was an asylum seeker, from Liberia. He had fled the country 10 months ago, arriving with a basic grasp of English. He'd worked hard over that time to learn English, and volunteered at the local church as well as a refugee centre. Imran enjoyed listening to him.

'So, you are nearly due a child. Your first?' Alexan asked, after Tony had informed him. 'This is a great adventure ahead of you.'

Imran nodded his head. 'Tony's told me what a headache I'm in for.'

They laughed.

'It is beautiful to watch your children grow. You will see.'

'Do you have family, Alexan?' asked Imran, unsure of whether he should pry.

Alexan's smile faded. 'Yes, they are back home, in Liberia. I have two boys and a girl. My wife is with them. They are very special to me. I miss them greatly. One day I hope to be able to play with them again, like these children are playing. I would like this.'

They'd cleared about halfway down the street when the news broke. Aliyah was going into labour. Imran had been checking in with her over the course of the day, and she'd had some pains but they were hoping it was just Braxton Hicks. But the contractions were becoming more frequent. This was the real thing. Imran had called the hospital, but there were no ambulances available.

'We'll have to get a midwife out to you. We'll let you know as soon as possible.'

A few minutes later the midwife phoned. 'I'm going to try to get out to you, Mr. Patel. Please tell Mrs. Patel not to panic. I'll be as quick as I can.'

'Please do something, Imran. Please.' Aliya's breathing was getting deeper.

'Give me a minute.' Imran rushed outside, and at the bottom of his drive was a small group of neighbours. They stood, sipping Mrs. Jones' tea, waiting for news.

'Everything alright, mate?' asked Tony.

'They can't send an ambulance out, and the midwife is a while away. What can I do?' Imran said.

He was speaking quickly and his voice was getting higher. He had to calm down if he was going to help Aliyah.

Jack put down his tea. 'I'll see if I can get the 4x4 over here.'

Imran thanked him and ran inside. A couple of minutes later there was a knock at the door. It was Mrs. Mahmood.

'My husband told me to come' she said, looking nervous.

Imran knew she didn't want to be here, but like her sons had been told to. Still, it was better than nothing. She sat with Aliyah, and began rubbing her back, talking to her. She looked anxious.

Imran checked outside. He could hear the revving of Jack's car in the distance, the slipping of tyres on the ice. It was not going to happen. All that work. Imran tried the midwife again; she was still a while away. Unlikely to arrive anytime soon. What could he do? Aliyah was bordering on hysterical and Mrs. Mahmood knew about as much as he did.

Just as he was about to sink into despair there was a knock at the door. He opened it, totally surprised at who he saw.

'Is that the midwife?' Aliyah shouted.

'No. It's Psy… I mean, Mrs. Sykes.'

Mrs. Sykes, wrapped in a faded, green velvet coat and a white wooly hat, glared at him. She barged past.

'Where's the lady? Right, stop looking like a frightened child and go get some towels. You, over there, close the door and boil some water, we haven't got all day. We need bowls and somebody get some blankets for Pete's sake.'

Mrs. Mahmood and Imran rushed about, trying to keep up with Mrs. Sykes' orders.

'Now then, young lady, you're going to have to be brave and strong, like I know you can be. You listen to my instructions carefully and follow them to the letter. Breathe when I tell you to breathe, and push when I tell you to push. Is that understood?'

Aliyah nodded, tears in her eyes. 'Yes, thank you.'

There was a knock at the door. 'Is everything ok?' Alexan asked.

A small crowd had grown behind him.

Mrs. Sykes shouted, 'Do you think you've got time for visitors, young man? Tell them to mind their own business and get back in here!'

Wide-eyed, Imran nodded and quickly shut the door.

Aliyah said later that the next fifteen minutes seemed to take an age, but they flew by for Imran. She screamed with every contraction, the pain making her grab Imran by the neck, pulling him towards her.

When their little girl was born, Aliyah collapsed into the cushions. Mrs. Sykes washed the baby and wrapped her in a towel, placing her in Aliyah's arms.

Imran's knees started to stiffen, then wobble. 'Thank you… thank you so…'

Aliyah raised her head to look at Mrs. Sykes and smiled.

Mrs. Sykes nodded, eyes warm. A knocking at the door called her away. The midwife had arrived.

MY FAVOURITE ROW

John Hindle

That black and white photograph,

the Primary was in its Centenary year,

children wore Victorian dress,

I took my dog with farmer's dress

and wondered what all the fuss was about,
eight cultures sharing class,
familiar roots over Darwen Tower,
over-looking all areas of ethnicity,
corner shops and yard bell,
all involved in the nativity play,
that playground of scrapped knees
and so many dreams,
childhood memories,
short trousers and warm coats
on cobbled streets in Community,
rows of garages and terrace streets,
memories of searching for four leaf clovers
on the green of what was a quarry,
the everlasting believe,
so many picked,
we were never disappointed,
penny sweets, football stickers and sherbet dips.

CONTRARY MARY

J PALMER

Illness in our family was seen as some sort of badness coming out. Since I was ill most of the time, I grew up thinking I must be extra bad. It became my claim to fame.

'It's all psychosomatic,' my aunt would say when I was gasping for breath, in the midst of an asthma attack. The remark jarred. Other people were allowed their bad backs or their indigestion. Why couldn't I have my asthma? It made me feel guilty or somehow to blame for my illness, as if I had invented it, just to spite my family. Maybe I had.

There were five children in our family and I was the middle one. I was the only one to have a middle name. That made me feel special. I was a 'boom baby ,' born after the Second World War, in the summer after the cold winter of 1947 when we got snowed up and cut off from the nearest village for weeks. Did the winter have anything to do with it? Was that why I felt that way? Born out of hardship, was that why I couldn't breathe?

Soon after I was born, my mother was pregnant again. She already had three children, two parents, and a husband to feed. The war was over, but there was still food rationing. We were getting free school milk and subsidised dinners but my mother couldn't help worrying. It was in her nature. The farm was going well but you never knew what might be round the corner. My mother saved the pennies and let the pounds take care of themselves.

Twice before the age of two, I was admitted to Blackburn Royal Infirmary suffering from acute bronchitis. I nearly died. My uncle John once told me a funny story about the second time I was admitted to hospital. I never knew if it was true or not. He had a vivid imagination. My father's shooting brake wasn't working, he said. Who was going to take me? My uncle was the only one with a car. Auntie Don, who lived next door to him, came along for good measure. They rushed me to the hospital.

'Are you the father of this child?' the doctor asked. Uncle John shook his head. The doctor turned to Auntie Don.

'Are you the mother of the child?' he asked.

'No,' said Auntie Don, adamantly. The very idea of it was preposterous. She had never been married. The doctor looked at Auntie Don. Auntie Don looked at Uncle John and then they all started laughing. After they had sorted things out with the doctor, they left me there. The nurses put me in an oxygen tent so I could breathe.

One day a man in a white coat came to see me. I remember him as being stiff and lifeless. He had no expression on his face. As he leaned over my bed I hid under the bedclothes and wouldn't speak. For years after, I had a recurrent dream about Guy Fawkes visiting me in hospital.

I liked the night times best in the hospital. The nurses stayed up on night duty, reading by lamplight, in case we cried out, wanting food or comfort. There was always someone there for you. I was sorry when they sent me home with the measles. I wasn't allowed to mix with the rest of the family in case I infected them. I had to go into 'quarantine' at Auntie Don's. By the time I got home three weeks later I had almost forgotten who my real mother and father were.

My recollections of the hospital became more and more vivid over time. The gloomy, Victorian building with its high windows was like a second home. There was one room I didn't like though. It was full of surgical instruments. In my mind it was all black. That was where I had my allergy tests. I sat on a cold, black, leather chair, feeling forlorn. It turned out I was allergic to everything: cat's fur, horse hair, sheep's wool, household dust, pollen, grass. How was I going to avoid all that, living on a farm?

But having survived the hospital experience I had a lifetime of anecdotes to tell.

'When I was in hospital,' I recounted later to my captive audience at home, 'I had a friend called Tommy Appy. We played together on a toy horse. It looked a bit like Muffin the Mule, but you could sit on it and it moved along when you jumped up and down on it.'

'You don't remember that,' my sister retorted. 'It's just what people have told you afterwards.'

'In hospital I had to drink out of a little teapot,' I said. 'And we had all sorts of toys to play with. '

The memories became more and more vivid as time went on. I clung to them as to a birthright.

'Don't treat her as an invalid,' the doctor said on my return home. This was often quoted at me.

I was beginning to hate that doctor. Didn't he realise what he had done? With that one pronouncement he had thwarted all my future efforts to get special treatment. Why couldn't he have kept his mouth shut? If it hadn't been for him, I might have got anything I wanted. Now I had to plead just to get my back rubbed or to have my milk brought in my own little, brown jug.

'But I am an invalid,' I protested. It didn't carry any weight. When I had an asthma attack I had to take a *Franol* pill. I hated the taste of those pills. They were bitter and they gave me the 'jitters' afterwards. I made the whole family shut their eyes while I took my pills. But I made sure they knew I was taking them.

It was my father who first coined the name 'Contrary Mary' for me.

'Mary, Mary. Quite contrary,

How does your garden grow?

With silver bells

And cockle shells

And cuttlefish all in a row.'

The rhyme didn't make any sense, but I knew why he had chosen to call me that.

MEMORY

Gideon Woodhouse

For I remember Bluebell Wood

With ground all carpeted in Spring

And when we dammed its gurgling brook

And hoped for Noah's flood.

And I remember building swings

With threadbare rope and half-snapped twigs.

I remember hunting newts

to save them from the new estate

And them escaping

To the Cat's delight.

And then, swift sliding down snow-topped hills

And drifts that came up to my waist

And riding prams with awful spills

And bikes o'er ramps that fell.

And I remember Bambi steps

On the new Olympic skating rink

And I remember feeling ill

After that first, forbidden drink.

That stolen kiss before the 19 bus

Then the joy of driving alone.

And I know these memories grow

Each day I live adds more and more

These all happened within my town

And yet there's still places to explore.

DANDELIONS AND NETTLES

Baron Jepson

Some of my fondest memories growing up are of a small terraced house, in a little place called *Waterfall* in Blackburn.

Playing with my matchbox car under the sideboard, I fall asleep. Waking I look up and marvel at the way it's constructed; so solid, made of wood with glue and screws. The carpet is not fitted; it is a carpet square, with a foot-wide gap from the skirting boards all around the room. No TV in the house or anyone else's we know. However, we are really posh as we have a twin-tub washing machine. Mum uses it to heat the water to fill the tin bath.

A small chest freezer under the stairs means we can store food really well now. Trying to catch a rat with mum and dad, we trap it behind the freezer. It is great fun. Moving the freezer we find it has gone. *God, they are fast!*

Love mum so much. I collect dandelions for her. She accepts them with love and a small giggle. Kissing my cheek, she tells me they are lovely. Placing them in a glass of water, *for that one day they will look perfect.*

Summer is hotter than I can remember. So many ladybirds, it is amazing. I have lots of nettle stings on my fingers and forearms as I have been collecting them. Mum gives me a glass jar. Placing the ladybirds lovingly inside, dad is explaining they need leaves to keep them alive, so I put some nettles in for them,

I can hear mum and dad giggling in the kitchen. They must love the ladybirds as well. They are really interesting. I never saw as many ever again.

Granddad owns the local newsagents and grocery shop. It is just around the corner from our house. I love looking through the window at all the wonderful things for sale. Granddad smells of Lions ointment and Germoline, with a caliper on his left leg. He is telling me it was from stopping a torpedo from hitting the ship during the war. Then he laughs. I think he already knows I don't believe him.

Grandmother is lovely. She is looking after me after an operation to remove my tonsils. She has given me dry toast, to remove the scabs from my throat. She is actually avoiding staring at me, as well as looking very uncomfortable.

I'm walking down a pavement of York-stone flags. It's lined with terraced houses, fancy green lampposts and the odd green box for the telephone wires.

'What happened to granddads leg, mum?' I ask, telling her what he said.

She is explaining granddad never went to war. He had an illness called polio, which is why we went to the health centre for a sugar lump.

Mum is telling me to be careful. Watch out - *stop!* I carry on walking backwards, watching her expression, gauging when, or if I should turn around. Too late… Turned around straight into a green lamppost. Mum reassures me I am brave, although crying.

It is at this point I feel confused; all the houses are starting to disappear.

Were they blown up during the war, mum?'

'No,' she laughed. 'They are knocking them down.'

'What for?'

She does not know. (Some of these areas are still undeveloped). But big changes are happening. The houses in our area, even the ones across the street, have been knocked down. It is exciting and strange.

Playing in a fantastic blue peddle car outside our house. It is very hard getting going on the cobbles, but determined to succeed I persevere. Peddling along, the back-alley becomes my destination. It is now cobbled with black stuff in between called tar. It is the first time I have seen this shiny black stuff. Getting out of the car I proceed to press and push at the black stuff, it is not long until I am modeling and making shapes. The smell is ok, in fact almost edible. It's disgusting! I cannot get it out of my mouth, it is stuck to my teeth, tongue and fingers. All over my blue car as well! I am trying to find something to wipe it on. Really upset, I look up to see Auntie Wendy and my mum laughing at me, through the back-yard gate. Chastising me, they take me in and clean me up.

The front door is made of wood, with an oval leaded glass panel at the top. I am playing in my blue car, with my rev-up Mickey Mouse bike. My favourite toy in the whole world! I am showing mum and dad how it can do *Evil Canevils,* off a lintel in the rubble across the street. Mum laughs and tells me to be careful.

'We are going to granddads. Come back and play outside the house, until we get back,' mum says.

I watch as they both get smaller, heading down the street.

Dad shouts, 'Don't shut the door!'

'Ok dad.'

Busy at play with my matchbox cars. I feel a sudden chill, looking up I realise there is nobody around. The area looks like a bombsite, strangely devoid of life. Most of the houses are knocked down now. I am suddenly very lonely. Hesitantly, I carry on playing with my cars.

In that instant the wind slams the door shut. Panic-stricken, I remember dad saying not to shut the door. What should I do? At that moment, mum and dad come around the corner, heading towards me. I cry, pleading with them, saying I am sorry. Dad is grumpy at first, but they soon see the funny side. Dad kicks the door open, then gives me some fruit and reassures me everything is ok. So I resume playing with my cars.

I never saw the Mickey Mouse rev-up bike again.

But the dandelions and nettles remained a part of me forever.

THE KING IS DEAD

Gideon Woodhouse

My cotton town, how do you feel?

Now that your King has lost his crown

His shuttles drawn, his looms laid down

Do you mourn your old liege, lord?

His spinning grasp on soul and board

Or do you feel he's in the mists?

His time no relevance to this

Or maybe mixture of the two?

Pride in’t past, but joy in the new

the knowledge that this town he made

That we are only here for him

But freed, no more slaved to his whim.

BLACKBURN

Thomas Eccles

When I look at my hometown of Blackburn, many opinions gather in my mind. It's a small town, quite unheard of in many other places, almost obscured in shade from the rest of the world. Some may catch a glimpse of it due to its football team, Blackburn Rovers. It's surrounded by many other smaller and larger towns and villages.

In a nutshell, I'm not really too sure what to think of this town.

When I look at Blackburn from a present point of view, it just seems empty, bleak and unfulfilling. The thing that gets to me the most is that I've heard people speak of how Blackburn was important in the Industrial Revolution. It was one of the first industrialized towns. Now, it seems so ridiculous to think this place was once a well known and inspiring place.

Looking at my hometown, I'm almost ashamed to even think that today, in my eyes; we have become almost nothing of importance. It seems that many have tried to replenish the status and efficiency of the town, but in doing so, have managed to destroy or rebuild over many historic landmarks and buildings that once stood proud.

Many people may read this with absolute disagreement to, but I don't actually hate my hometown, I just feel that we have become a ghost town in the light of what we used to be.

SOME HOVIS AND A CUP OF OXO

Diane Smith

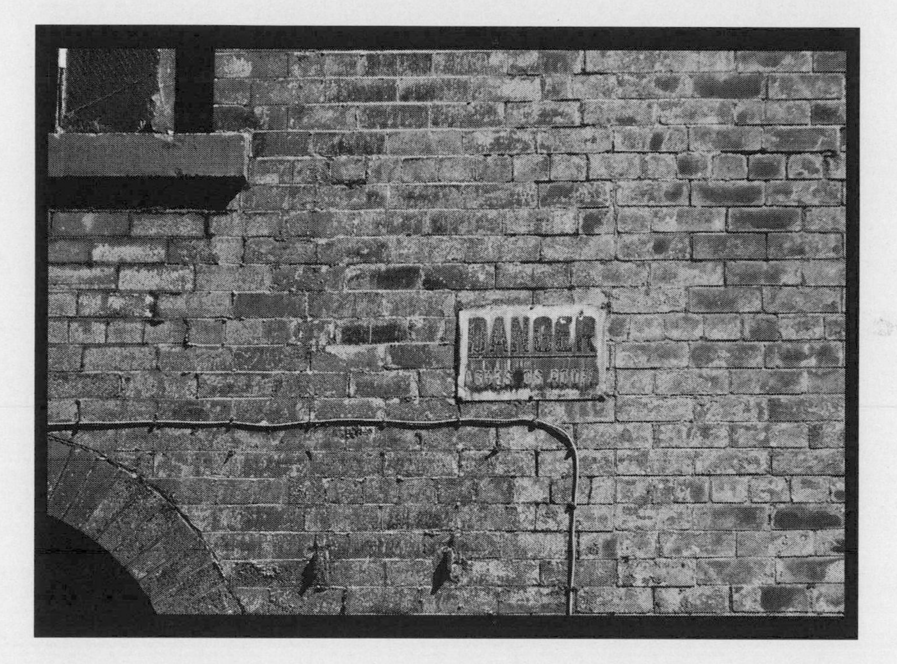

Alice hated Grandma's house; it smelled funny. Grandma smelled funny. How Alice loathed the trip to Blackburn with her mother. It took all day travelling from London's Victoria coach station up the A1 with a stop at Grantham, then on to Birmingham. Alice had usually been sick by the time she arrived in the Midlands, much as she tried to suppress it for several miles before accepting the lost cause.

Longfield Street was barren. No trees anywhere; rows and rows of houses with tiny back yards. Grim and cold, but at least no traffic.

At some level Alice knew her grandmother was really a kindly woman, always in laughing good spirits. But Grandma was so *old,* so hunched over and shrunken, wearing those noisy black clogs. The lino did little to muffle the sound and the stone flags in the kitchen made the clog's irons ring out with every step. Alice thought the heavy footwear must help to keep tiny Grandma standing upright, weighing her feet down so she did not fall.

Grandma's grey hair was thick and unruly, like wire wool. She wore drab clothes under a floral pinafore, with a bib and skirt that covered the dullness beneath. Alice noticed the thick stockings slumped in wrinkles around Grandma's ankles.

What was more disturbing, Grandma talked funny and Alice had trouble understanding what she said. Alice had at last come to recognise that 'childer' referred to youngsters. They all talked funny here and her aunts' booming voices were particularly terrifying. At least Grandma spoke quietly, whereas Alice's aunts always shouted.

They made free with their hands to ruffle her hair and pinch her cheeks. Even Alice's mother would not touch her in such a familiar way. It made Alice droop her shoulders and pull into herself without actually moving off the spot. But she could never get away from their advances.

'Have her hair cut,' said Aunt Annie from her chair next to the black range. She had just filled the sooty kettle and placed it on the hob. 'It's sapping her strength.'

Alice liked her hair the length it was and her stomach knotted as she scowled, tipping her head down.

Aunt Mary's bustling entry broke the tension. She was breathless and rushed as usual. 'I've got something for you,' she said to Alice as she took her coat off.

Alice was intrigued by the small brown paper bag that weighed heavily as she took it from Aunt Mary's cold hands. The bag contained a pair of child's clogs in red leather. They were too small for Alice, and would have fitted a toddler.

Alice immediately imagined her baby brother wearing the little shoes. He was 'down south ,' as the aunts referred to her home. Although she knew Blackburn was 'up north ,' that indefinable part of the map, she had not appreciated that her home was as indistinct to them as 'up north' was to her.

Alice fell in love with the clogs immediately and they caused her to consider Grandma's footwear in a new light. Her own shoes were always 'for school ,' so red footwear, even if too small, was an unexpectedly valuable gift. She could already see the jealousy on her classmates' faces when she showed the clogs to the other girls next term.

The door opened again admitting a wave of cold air alongside Uncle Charlie. Alice liked his cheeky way with everyone. He made the whole family laugh, even managing to get a smile from her mother.

The small front room, one of two downstairs rooms, was already bursting with family members by the time Charlie arrived. No one seemed to notice they were crammed in tightly and Alice was surprised at how they kept piling in. Uncle Charlie on his own could fill a whole room with his presence.

'Let's buy some pies for dinner,' he said to Alice, laughing as he grabbed her hand and propelled her out of the front door. She grabbed her coat quickly on the way out.

As they strolled, Uncle Charlie sang right through Eddie Cochran's 'Three Steps to Heaven ,' which Alice knew from the hit parade. Once they reached the corner pie shop, Alice could see it was already packed with workers on their midday break. 'Two meat and potato and one whimberry,' said Uncle Charlie. Alice observed his relaxed way of chatting with people in the queue.

'We would never do that in the fish and chip shop back home,' she thought. Everyone there was a stranger. 'Don't talk to strangers.'

She knew they must be ignored. But here everyone seemed like family. It felt odd, but she liked the friendly atmosphere in the warm, moist pie shop. She watched the condensing water droplets from the steam running in rivulets to pool on the window sills.

As she watched Uncle Charlie, Alice smiled at his cheeky antics with the woman serving. The heavy accent took their conversation over her head, but she knew they must be talking about her.

Back to Grandma's and a return to that smell; a mixture of gas, old lino and coal. And old people. Alice nibbled at a piece of pie. She had really wanted it on the way down the street, but once in the house her hunger evaporated. She dreaded the meal's finale. Tea with sterilised milk. 'Steri' they called it cheerily, as if it was the only possible milk in the world. How could they drink it?

Alice thought it unfortunate that she and her mother had to stay with Aunt Annie, although she loved the night time spectacle of Blackburn's lights seen from the top of Buncer Lane. One morning Aunt Annie had even poured 'steri' on Alice's cereals.

'No, thank you,' said Alice, with a tinge of disgust in her voice that was hard to hide.

What with the smells and strong flavours Alice found herself saying, 'No, thank you,' to food until she nearly starved. But no amount of starvation could overcome the smells in that house.

After dinner, Alice's mother put her coat on, picked up her brown crocodile skin handbag and made to follow Aunt Mary out of the door. 'Come on, Alice. Say goodbye to Grandma.'

Alice was relieved to be going at last. 'Auntie Mary wants you to see where she works Alice,' her mother said, pursing her lips.

Aunt Mary seemed agitated and wanting to get on.

'I must get back. I've taken too long already, Joan,' Aunt Mary said to Alice's mother.

Alice saw the dark outline of the mill as they approached. Drawing closer, the building towered above them. As her aunt pushed open the door to the mill Alice could hear a frenzy of noise. Alice's aunt disappeared down a corridor while her mother stopped to speak to a man in a tiny glass cubicle just inside the front door.

Something seemed to have been agreed and her mother propelled Alice towards a pair of double doors.

Once they pushed open the doors to the weaving shed, the sound washed over Alice, drowning her and nearly stopping her breath. It was impossible to hear her mother's voice as she struggled to explain something. The noise stifled Alice's thoughts and made her head swim.

Her mother nodded to some of the women as she and Alice squeezed their way past rows of machinery until they reached Aunt Mary. She was overseeing several looms, busying herself with each in turn and moving swiftly between them and concentrating on tasks Alice did not understand.

She watched her aunt gesticulate in signs, mouthing words to the other weavers. Alice could not fathom the strange, silent conversation; another language. She had seen enough and thought her ears would never recover. The noise was terrifying and the looms were demanding monsters.

She was relieved when they were outside once more, but relief was short lived. Now they were off to visit Aunt Kitty, a long bus ride, up, up, up to Shadsworth.

'You talk funny,' Alice informed her two cousins as they played in the road near Aunt Kitty's house.

'No we don't. *You* do.'

Alice was adamant; she would not even consider this a remote possibility. The argument raged before they finally concentrated on their marbles in the gutter as the daylight faded.

The next day met with more 'No thank yous,' from Alice until Uncle Bill, Aunt Mary's husband, stopped by with real milk for Alice's cereals. They called it 'cow's milk ,' as if it was something unusual. He also bought her a 'Diana' comic and Alice warmed to this dusty-eyed coalman.

Back to Granma's for the afternoon and a never-ending stream of people in and out. They were curious about herself and her mother, staring at them both too boldly, Alice thought.

Her stomach was making its empty presence felt. Too many 'No thank yous,' but she could not help herself. It was easier to say than 'Yes please.' Alice's hunger was growing by the time Joanne breezed into her grandmother's house, a girl a few years older than Alice.

'I'm getting tea ready for everyone coming home,' Joanne said. 'Do you want to come and help?'

Alice surprised herself by agreeing to go. Wasn't Joanne a stranger to be avoided? They crossed the road into another tiny house. But Joanne's house did not smell like Grandma's.

'Would you like some bread and marge?' Joanne asked.

Alice regarded the offering. The Hovis smelled good and the margarine did not really smell at all.

'Yes, please,' she ventured, bolting the two slices.

'Like some more?' asked Joanne.

'Yes, please,' answered Alice with relish. She was on a roll and several slices disappeared in quick succession.

'And a cup of Oxo?'

The contents of the cup vanished as fast as the slices of bread.

Alice smiled warmly for the first time in days.

MEDIOCRITY IS NOT ENOUGH

David R Morgan

I pursue decades of obscure study

and publish nothing.

The drunk reads maps of the skies

under which he sleeps,

and like the stars he is remote.

In the eight-hundred section
the drunk lectures me on Barbara Castle.

I sigh and offer unrealistically
to trade my tie for his bottle,
leather for his tattered tennis shoes.

Ignoring me, he reads in a scratchy
bass from The Yellow Submarine Lyrics.

Neither of us is content.
Neither can be.
That is the point.

Outside, bundles of books in hands,

we watch clouds roll across Lancashire.

All I see is rain.

Rubbing his weary eyes, he sees 5000 holes

filled with locusts, angels, artillery.

BLACKBURN LIBRARY

Lotte Gracie Neil

Books. Hundreds and hundreds of books, adventure, sci-fi, music. I have a good view of the children's library; now I suppose I must describe where I live...

From the wall, I can see almost everything here - God knows what lies out of those shiny doors that people disappear in and out of so regularly. The books are brightly coloured and are never, ever dusty, for they are removed and replaced so often, the only thing that gathers dust is me. Glimmering and buzzing strangely, (next to the assorted book cases) are the 'computers' (I think that's what they're called), on which I gaze at images that flash before my painted eyes. I don't understand computers. I overheard one person naming a little oval-shaped object next to them a mouse! It doesn't even have a nose, or whiskers.

From here, I can see dozens of sticky little children, all letting off a strong odor of sweets, and huge towering men crouching down to find a book they remember from long ago. The library is warm, and an energy seems to seep from its walls, casting a peaceful atmosphere of quiet study. The sheer wonderfulness of my home sends me into paroxysms of delight - even though I cannot move anyway - and when I read over children's shoulders, the characters seem so tangible, I can almost feel them. Harry Potter, speeding on his Firebolt, Oliver Twist, pick-pocketing, even Max, searching for The Wild Things. Oh how I long to meet them! Are they real?

When I read, I can feel the tension, the excitement, the horror, thriving away inside me, and I can feel myself sucked into the book, but then some careless child shuts the book with a 'SNAP!' and I want to shout 'Hey! Can't you see I was reading that?'

My fellow paintings, (Thomas The Tank Engine, Fluffy the Dog and the Iron Man) feel much the same as me, but at night, when the lights are out, the people gone, the warmth drained, we can tell what we've read till we're hoarse.

THE TROUBLE WITH BLACKBURN

Christine Clayton

'I'm not living here!' I always say, crossing the Cathedral Close. 'It's freezing.'

Yet I would – live here, I mean. Sometimes it frightens me to realise how much I want to.

I cannot miss the Cathedral. Every visit I must step inside the door and stop. How could anywhere feel so right? Look so perfect?

All this began with a dream, one year, in the month of June. I'm a good dreamer, and for years have kept a log of my best efforts. But even I had never dreamt of Blackburn, never *been* to Blackburn, never had anything to *do* with Blackburn.

Nevertheless, there I was in the dream, apparently at ease with an unknown family in Blackburn. It was all so vivid.

I spent, perhaps, more time poring over maps and considering what I called 'this Blackburn business' than a woman of balanced mind should. These mysterious people, I concluded, must be Dad's. Of my mother's assorted relatives I had been all too aware as a little girl, but of my father's I had known nothing.

Then the haunting started. Everywhere I went, Blackburn appeared: letters, pictures, acquaintances, book characters – even tradesmen's vans – seemed to bring the name to me – or was it just something I suddenly noticed?

One February day, I finally decided to go – more for curiosity than anything. I stared down from the station platform at the haphazard mixture of old and new, beautiful and prosaic, spread out before me. Half-ashamed of having travelled from the other end of Lancashire on the strength of a dream.

People walked, I found, through the Cathedral grounds to the shops, so I did the same and felt, in the very bricks and paving stones, Blackburn's past, still with her.

Suppose I try the Library, then, for this pretend family? It was a game; I was going to laugh and forget it. But they were there, waiting for me, in that room where the books have been well and truly loved, and the lady at the desk doesn't mind if you touch things, or giggle, or cry, or have a 'Hurray!' moment, or plonk down on the floor.

Were they mine, these storybook people, owners of a cotton mill and my father's name? It wouldn't be true just because I wanted it to be. Wanted? *Why* did I want it to be? Tea, I thought, was necessary.

Squeezed into the hot café with the old-fashioned tills, the voices like music around me, I tried to read. But I was staring out at the shabby street.

I love the bricks of the old buildings; I love the sudden bursts of sculpture; I love the odd characters; I love the scent – usually chips; I love the biting wind across the Boulevard; the severity of a certain steep, terraced street near the Park; I love red brick and grey slate on a murky, rainy day; the way the houses climb the hill on the north side; that brooding look; that view from the Park.

Wait. Think. Consider. But it's too late.

Gradually, they have revealed themselves to me, my family: Great, Great Grandpa, tall, vigorous, kindly and clever, who wanted to be a doctor but went into the Mill, and grew up to build his own mills; Great Grandpa, businessman, sportsman, churchman, gentleman; Grandpa, Corporation Clerk. They have bequeathed me a place to belong to.

A place that doesn't pretend: not pretty, but beautiful; not perfect, but loveable.

BAG LADY

Martin McAreavey

She glides with an air of resigned destitution.

A once stately stay-at-home, now a shambolic pile

A Sainsbury Heiress, no less –

Bags deployed as ballast

Behind her thoughts of might have been…

No longer the beautiful wife

No more the dutiful hostess

Her time is spent in long, contemplative

Stares into days and nights gone by.

The leaves roll disdainfully around

her ball gown exquisite footwear

holed, unheeled and unwhole;

Protection only from the stares of uncaring unseeing

passersby who think only, 'Bag Lady.'

'detritus of our society,' Relic of some long forgotten trust

Here today, just. Here tomorrow? Who cares?

She sits now, enthroned on her favourite low wall;

Regal, Resting, Rough and Unready

And waits for rescue.

Waiting still. She's wasting forever –

Her hero now not tall, dark and dashing

But more inclined to the snap of cheap gin sans tonique.

Exotic. Final. Floundering,

She shuffles busily off…

SUNDAY MORNING BY BLACKBURN LOCKS

Gaye Gerrard

He sits, slumped, precariously balanced on a bollard, his clothes stained. I stand alone at the tiller and, as our boat rises on the in-rushing water, the stench of stale alcohol drifts towards me.

Through glazed eyes he stares at me hazily, lifting an almost empty quart bottle in his dirty, trembling hand. In the other is a mobile phone into which, with much eff-ing and blinding, he is demanding more cider, from someone unseen. The stare becomes a glare as I draw level with him. The throbbing engine is doing his head in, he tells me.

'Eff off!'

I wish I had a choice, but I am stuck in the lock. He snarls only feet from my face as, holding my breath I wait for the lock gates to be opened by my husband.

It's a relief to be out of reach of the towpath, where lads in hoods stand, with lowered heads, taking deep breaths from cupped hands. Muttering furtive words, they raise their faces with vague smiles and gaze at the sky which looks thick with smoke.

But then a bright and beautiful moment; in a shaft of light four Muslim ladies, in salwar kameez, come jogging in a line towards us, pleased to be out and keeping fit.

We smile, and wave, and part.

THE METHODIST CHAPEL

Alan Taylor

Dry leaves swept by the wind

form puddles of brown in front of

graffiti scarred entrance doors.
Rusty railings encompass grounds
thick with stunted grass and
trailing arms of blackened briar.
This grim monument erected as
testimony to the mill workers' faith
abandoned; the 'For Sale' sign
nailed to its pockmarked wall
peeling long strips of paint.
Around the Chapel terraced houses
spill, onto grey uneven pavements,
children, lovers and elderly folk
who, as in time-lapse photography,
form streams of staccato images,
the Chapel a silent, lonely island
in the midst of bustle and noise.

"A DAY IN THE LIFE OF A YOUNG PERSON"

Everyone knows that when people get old they always go on about when they were young. They go on about how bad their lives were and how they had to do everything in the house. They always complain about how young people are so advantaged and spoilt, and they love using the well known phrase, 'back in my day'. I want to change this. I want to let the older generation know about what we young people struggle with in life. I want them to know what we feel positive about and what we would like to do with our lives. That's why I am going to tell you a story about a day in the life of living in Blackburn.

Well, where to start. I wake up in the morning to a cold, frosty window. Mum as usual is shouting, 'Get up, you're going to be late for college'. So I run downstairs grabbing a piece of toast and run out the door to the bus stop. When at the bus stop I seem to wait for hours in the cold, and by the time the bus comes it feels like I've been waiting for so long, I've turned into an ice sculpture. That's if the bus even arrives on time.

The bus is the next problem; you get on the bus and try to find a seat. That's after you have paid some extortionate price to feel like you are some farmer's cattle on the way to the slaughter house. While on the bus you get pushed and shoved, side to side, back and forth, up and down. The old people are having a moan about how fast the bus driver is going. I don't know why, at least they are sat down! Not like me. I am being squashed by twenty other people trying not to fall on the floor. I always think if someone falls we will all fall down, like a line of dominoes.

After jumping off the bus you start rushing to college to get there before 9 o'clock. You should see all of the college students that get off the buses and rush off to college in the rain. They rush like it's some type of race, running across the road, jumping over puddles, and fighting with their umbrellas because of the mighty wind. We all look like half-dead zombies, so tired they haven't bothered having a wash or looking in the mirror. We young people always have our hair everywhere, but we just say it's the latest fashion.

On arrival to college I remember that I have an exam and two pieces of coursework that need handing in today. I think, What to do? What excuse should I use this time? But I soon get over the panic when I see my friends and I just start talking to them. At college the day starts off dull and uninteresting with boring lessons and lectures. After a while of listening to the coffee-breath lecturer, it's lunch time. But that's not the most interesting thing in my life; it's a hard job looking for something good to eat on a student's budget.

In town the pushing and shoving continues for everyone, rushing to get something to eat. I think to myself, What do I fancy today? Gregg's is always a cheap option but the queues are always so long. There's Hampson's around the corner but that's the same. What about McDonalds? No, it's too expensive for something so little and the queue is even longer. In fact, it goes out of the door. If you ever get served in McDonalds there is never anywhere to sit and chill out. I'll get something from the market. Then again, they act stuck up and their food is so bland. Looks like it's Tesco again. Can't go wrong with their cheap and cheerful meal deal for only £2.00.

That's dinner over with. Back to college now, mental note to self remember to go the long way back to college. I don't feel in the mood today to get hassled off people trying to sell me something, or the big issue woman shouting in my ear to buy a magazine off her. I just want to walk back to college with no hassle and no one asking me questions about my age. This afternoon at college I have that massive test; this is one of the tests that go to my final mark. This is the last test of the year. I hate doing tests, because you have to wait forever to get the results. Hope I have revised enough so I can go off to university and then hopefully get a good job to make mum proud.

I am back at college now and there's seconds to go before the exam. I am getting so nervous. Starting to sweat and forgetting everything that I have revised. Hope I don't fail, Hope I don't fail, Hope I don't fail, keeps repeating in my head. I go blank and start to write on my exam paper.

3, 2, 1, finished the exam is over. Done. I hope that all of the questions were answered correctly, and I hope that I did enough to pass this exam. Well, I won't find out for another few months.

That's another day at college out of the way. Time to go back into town and look for something new to wear. Primark here I come. When in Primark there are so many things to choose from but one big thing that holds me back is they never have size. Every time I go up to a store assistant I always ask them if they could look in the back for my size. They always come out with the same thing, We only have what's on the shelves. I think they are either saying it because they can't be bothered or because they are discriminating because of my age. Oh well, I don't care. I can save money by not buying anything this time.

I just remembered it's Youth Action tonight. I love being involved in the sessions at Youth Action. Mostly because you are able to do lots of different things, for example the Remembrance Parade or even the Personal Safety course that I have just completed. Tonight is the chill out session, where I am able to watch videos on YouTube, or even play on the Nintendo Wii with my friends. I feel that when I am at Youth Action all the stresses of live fade away and everything feels relaxed. I think there should be more things like Youth Action because it gives young people the chance to learn something new. Plus you can talk to people about problems that you may have.

That's it. Day finished, time for bed. You see, that older generation tells young people like me that their lives were hard. But I think that our lives are different, but just as hard. I couldn't imagine being a young person sixty years ago but I can say from experience that a young person today has a hard life. We have to study a lot to try to get a good job and that's if there are any jobs for us when we've finished studying. Then there's nothing for us to do in the evening or at weekends. No wonder people always hear about so many young people resorting to either drinking alcohol, or getting into trouble with the police.

Shane McHugh (Youth Action)

NORTHERN STREET

Keith Dalton

Snow dances in the pale sun,

it falls and gathers in the corners

of salt white streets.

Wind chills the newspaper stand.

I buy some local news and take my

change from a coin stained hand of

an old man who stamps his feet, and

wishes for gas fired heat in his three rooms

of living in a steep northern street.

Low Sun

Old woman in low sun,

with a white loaf in a cheap carrier bag,

shuffles past the sudden burst of colour

coughed up by wild flowers

on the brown scrub of wasteland,

where rows of terraced houses

once spewed out the human cogs and wheels

that ran the mills and factories.

She stops for breath,

And looks across the flat empty streets,

where young boys dare with mountain bikes

over the rough ground,

in the mundane drift of nothing in particular.

Moon Rises

Day moon rises,

Old hurt rage.

I walk most days along the canal

And skirt the town when leaves push,

And the wind bites enough to need a top coat.

Water ripples where the wind glides.

Memory works, fades, and returns

Full of a life that can snap,

And leave a broken sky half-full of clouds

That's long in time and early April.

The leaves push,

The wind bites enough to need a top coat.

Day moon rises,

Old hurt rage.

"SATURDAY NIGHTS"

In the early 60s my mates and I looked forward to going 'Up the Mirabelle' on Saturday nights. It was well known for good records and good dancers, (I should say good Boppers). There were other dance halls in Blackburn but we liked this one the best. The lads were 16 to about 19 yrs old and they would have their Italian suits on and shoes with pointed toes. Their hair either a short crew cut, or a big quiff like Cliff or Elvis. We girls had at least two sticky-out net underskirts worn under swirling skirts or dresses. Or a smart pencil skirt with a fine cardi worn back to front, which was the fashion. 15 denier nylons, American Tan was the shade, and white stiletto shoes. We all loved to use semi-permanent rinses on our hair in various shades. My favourite, being a brunette, was Black Tulip. Our hair was backcombed to within an inch of its life, then styled, then sprayed with Bellair lacquer, until a gale-force eight wouldn't shift it.

Sometimes we would use a silver or gold hairspray just at the front, or maybe the fringe, but we gave this up when we realised our partners weren't too happy to have silver lapels, or chins. Nearly time to come out of the cloakroom, just a quick dab of Coty L'Amaint or Pico's Pagan. The Drifters, Gene Vincent, Little Richard. The music was great; we girls were in our element.

There was no bar so the lads would have their hands stamped 'Pass-out' and go to the Balaclava pub five minutes away. It was usually after ten when they returned in good spirits, ready for a good bopping session. At 11pm, after the last smooch, the long walk home. The streets would be full of people coming out of the pubs and other dance halls. We usually queued for chips and ate them out of the newspaper wrappings, vinegar dripping out the bottom. When reaching our street, I would take off my high heels, usually laddering my nylons, so my mum and dad wouldn't waken and know it was just past midnight. I never succeeded in this. They always knew exactly what time I got in.

Pauline Jackson

EGGSHELLS

A. J. Ashworth

We loaded up the car with suitcases full of shorts, T-shirts and thin summer shoes. Then I sat on the windowsill while Joel kicked a ball against the wall. Grandma came out panting, with her handbag and a plastic carrier swinging from her arm like huge bangles.

'Come on,' she said, her cheeks bright pink from the heat. 'Let's be off then.'

'Have we got anything to eat on the way?' said Joel, spinning the ball on his middle finger like a basketball player.

She lifted the carrier up. 'Yes.'

'Give us a clue,' he said.

'Food,' she said and got in the back, sitting in the middle.

Joel threw the football at my head and caught it again. I kicked out at him but he dodged out of the way.

'Stop it, or you can forget the caravan,' said Dad.

Mum shooed me and Joel into the car. 'Yes, come on,' she said. 'Don't start being silly now.'

Grandma fanned herself with the newspaper. 'Let's hope we can get there quick,' she said. 'I feel like a sardine already.'

We moved off.

'Sardine?' said Joel. 'Can I have something to eat?'

Dad glanced around. 'No. We're only just getting going.'

'I'm hungry,' Joel said, bouncing the ball on his knee.

Dad turned the radio on.

'It's too hot in here,' Grandma said, wiping at her forehead and reaching over to wind the window down. 'I can't stand it. Let's have some fresh air in.'

'Well don't let it get too draughty,' said Dad. 'It kills my neck.'

A hearse went past in the next lane, its body black and shiny as a beetle. There were two men in the front dressed in dark suits - behind them a coffin with flowers around its side. The driver was laughing hard while the other just stared at him with his mouth open in a smile.

'Oh, God,' said Grandma. 'That's all we need.'

'Well hopefully we won't be seeing the inside of one of those for a while,' said Mum.

'Let's hope not,' said Dad.

'Just look.' Grandma put a hand up to her throat. 'They should show some respect.'

The hearse turned off and I picked up my book from the side of the seat. It was a collection of war poetry from school and was filled with the sounds of shells and guns; the filthy smell of the trenches; how it felt to see your friends killed.

Joel punched at the cover and it fell from my hands.

'Don't start, you, or we won't be going anywhere,' said Grandma and hit him on the side of the head.

'Who's starting?' said Dad, looking in the rear view mirror. 'Who's starting?'

Joel slumped back in the seat and rolled the football up and down his thighs. Grandma tutted then began doing the crossword with Mum. I straightened the book in my lap but left it where it was, listening to the radio instead. There was a Madonna song on: *If we took a holiday, took some time to celebrate.* I put my head against the window and started to drift off but woke when the newsreader said a man had died after falling from a rollercoaster.

'Awful,' said Mum. 'What a way to go.'

‘There are some horrible things in the world,’ said Grandma. ‘It makes you think.’

Joel flung himself back against the seat. ‘Think what? Can we have something else on?’

‘Shush, Joel-baby,’ said Grandma, opening up the plastic bag on her knee. ‘Put one of these in your cake-hole.’ She handed him a ham sandwich on white bread.

Dad put his hand back towards her without saying anything. She gave him a sandwich too and before long food was being passed around to everybody. I got a boiled egg with the shell still on. I tapped it against the window until a web of cracks appeared then I started to peel the shell off.

‘Have you got any crisps?’ said Joel. ‘I could just eat some.’

Dad turned around, taking his eyes off the road, and hit my brother softly on the leg. ‘Stop it now. I’m not listening to this all the way there. I’ll turn back first.’

‘Al,’ said Mum.

‘Well.’

Joel put his head on Grandma’s shoulder and an arm around her waist.

‘Oh, here we go,’ she said, smiling.

'You know I love you, Gran.'

'Creep,' I said, eating the soft, still warm egg and looking out at a light rain. Cars were getting all glittery from the wet and their windows speckled with drops. It was hard to see the people inside because of the grey rain and the spray from the road. I looked back at Joel who was now squeezing Grandma's waist and giving her a kiss on the arm.

She laughed. 'You little so-and-so,' she said, rustling into the bag and handing him a pack of ready salted.

'Thanks,' Joel said, pulling away from her and grabbing for the bag.

'Pig,' said Dad, shaking his head. 'Nothing but a little pig.'

Before long we were out of Blackburn and on the motorway. There were lots of cars going the same way, most of them steamed up from the people inside. The rain was getting heavy by then and the movement of the windscreen wipers made me think of the metronomes we had at school – sweeping right and left, right and left until they made you feel tired. I yawned and turned away, looking down at the wet road and seeing how the wheels splashed through and water sprang away from the backs of them.

'Hold on,' said Dad, and we all jolted forward as he pressed on the brakes. 'Accident I think. Everyone's slowing up.'

'That's all we need,' said Mum.

I put my face up against the glass to try and see. Mum was doing the same in the front. Dad turned off the radio.

'The only thing I can see is a car on the hard shoulder and a wagon in front of it with its hazards on,' she said. 'Nothing else.'

Grandma started to squeeze up against me as she tried to get a better view. Joel leaned over too and dug his hand into my thigh.

I pushed at his arm. 'That hurts,' I said. He dug it in a little further before moving it. His eyes were all wide as he tried to see through the rain.

'Can you see anything yet?' said Grandma. 'I can't see a thing.'

'Just the car and the wagon,' I said. 'It looks as if it's on a slant.'

We got a bit closer. Everyone around us had slowed down too. There were drivers and passengers all doing the same things we were; leaning over each other, tilting heads, trying to see what was going on. As we got nearer to the car I could see it was lifted up at the back where it had a half-flat wheel. A new wheel was leaning against the bumper but there was nobody around trying to change it or anyone standing waiting for help. From somewhere behind us I heard sirens.

'The police are here,' said Dad. 'Ambulance as well. Must be something bad.'

I looked back and saw them coming, their lights pulsing out like blue heartbeats.

'What's going on?' asked Joel. 'Is somebody dead or something?'

'Oh, Joel, I hope not,' said Grandma. 'Don't say that for goodness sake.' Her hand was back at her throat.

Joel's eyes were sparkling now and his mouth open as if he was hungry for something. There was a half-eaten apple in his lap. 'Can you see what's happened?' he said. 'Mum?'

'No,' she said. 'Nothing.'

I pressed up against the glass again as we moved into another lane, out of the way of the wagon.

'Anything yet?' said Joel.

I stared at the blue sheeting on the side of the wagon then looked beneath. There was a crumpled mass wrapped in folds of dirty fabric at the back of the twin wheels near the cab; a body twisted at a strange angle and tangled up in a summer dress and raincoat like a mummy in pastel-coloured bandages.

It was a woman. I could see her long, red hair like wet corkscrews half over her face and half on the road beneath. My heart thumped hard in my chest as I caught sight of her head partly open on one side, as if a scoop had been taken from it and a red hole left open to the air.

Grandma gasped. 'Oh, look away,' she said.

I turned to her and she had a hand over her mouth.

'Don't look,' said Mum.

'Poor woman,' said Grandma. 'The poor woman.'

'What happened?' said Joel. 'What happened?'

Dad put his hand on Mum's leg. 'I don't know,' he said. 'She must have been trying to change the wheel or something.' He watched us in the rear view mirror. 'Looks like she's been dragged under by the wagon.' He shook his head. 'It's terrible. Don't you two ever do that when you're older – change a wheel on a motorway.'

'No, don't you dare,' said Mum.

‘God bless her,’ said Grandma. ‘God rest her soul.’

When we got past the wagon I didn’t want to look outside anymore. Even Joel stopped trying to see out. After a while Dad turned the radio back on but quieter than before. I picked up my book and tried to concentrate on the lines but couldn’t. I kept seeing the woman’s hair and her twisted body.

Joel leant onto his football and looked forward into the rain slapping down on the windscreen. Sometimes he said things like, ‘Her head was smashed in,’ or ‘She was all twisted up.’ But he fell silent as soon as Grandma cupped a hand at the back of his head or rubbed him in circles on his back.

Nobody said anything much for the rest of the journey and we made it to the caravan site an hour or so later. The place was as empty as if it was winter and there only seemed to be a few families around, most of them locked away inside the rows of dirty white vans.

It rained a lot during those first days so me and Joel went to the amusement arcade each morning but the games didn’t seem to last long. We were soon back at the caravan, pockets empty, trying to play tennis inside with the bats and soft balls Grandma had bought for us.

One morning when the sun shone though, Dad waved two buckets at us.

'Do you want to go cockling?' he said.

Joel snatched a bucket and ran for the steps down to the beach. I took mine, slipped my pink jelly shoes on and followed.

We went out far along the bay, the sea sparkling along the horizon like a glittery worm. We couldn't remember what to do so we copied Dad; took off our shoes, trod our feet into the sand until it squelched and softened, and when we felt the bumps beneath our toes we dug our fingers in and pulled out the gritty heart-shaped cockleshells. We swished them in the little pools of seawater that had formed then dropped them into our buckets.

As Dad and Joel moved further on up the beach I dug and uncovered a family of five cockles nestled close together. I was about to shout after them to tell them, my heart thudding hard at the discovery, but as I placed the tiny humped backs side by side in the bucket something didn't feel right: I kept thinking about their frightened little bodies inside and imagined them calling out to each other in a language I didn't understand. So I put them back in the slush, along with the others I'd dug up, and covered them with a handful of sand.

Instead of searching for more I used my big toe to write 'Help' in huge letters so that someone flying over might see. But I didn't see any planes – not even far off ones. And for a while I felt as if there was only me around.

After a while Dad and Joel came back. 'I'm bored now,' said Joel. 'Can we go?'

'Come on then grumpy,' said Dad. Then he peered into my bucket. 'You haven't got any.'

'I didn't feel like it,' I said.

Dad nodded and touched the top of my head. Then we followed our footsteps back, the sun nipping at our bare arms. We hardly spoke. Instead I just listened to the clink and roll like marbles in Joel's bucket, as he swung it backwards and forwards at his side.

The day after, when the cockles had been soaked and boiled, Dad picked them, placed them in a bowl and sprinkled them with vinegar. Joel grabbed a handful and chewed them with his mouth open as if they were gum.

'Well done you lot,' said Grandma, putting three or four in her mouth at once. 'They're lovely.'

Mum ate them one at a time. 'Nice,' she said, then put one in front of my face. 'Are you not having any?'

I shook my head. 'No, they're disgusting. They look like little aliens.'

Mum frowned. 'You've eaten them before.'

'I can't now,' I said, shuddering. 'Look at them.'

Joel leaned over and opened his mouth so I could see them all crushed up on his tongue. 'Yummy,' he said, thrusting it in and out.

'Joel,' said Mum. 'Don't be dirty.'

Grandma laughed and Dad sighed.

I turned away and closed my eyes. I felt queasy at the thought of them, biting down on the greasy, cold flesh. They were like decayed teeth with a strange yellow bit like a foot sticking out. I imagined one of them coming alive and tickling my tongue. 'They're horrible,' I said. 'I don't know how you can eat them.'

'Easy,' said Joel. 'Easy peasy lemon squeezy.' And he grabbed another handful and pushed them into his mouth.

When it came for us to be coming home a couple of days later, I don't remember much about it – except that the roads seemed shorter somehow, as if the world had shrunk from all the rain. I think Dad told us a joke when we got near to where the accident happened but Mum and Grandma just groaned instead of laughing. Joel and I stayed quiet and kept staring over as if we expected to still see the woman lying there. But none of us spoke about it. It was almost as if we were holding our breath, counting to ten, until we were safely past.

What I do remember was finding bits of eggshell on the back seats and picking them up and crunching them against my nails. I think I was finding them for weeks after; sharp curves of pinky-brown that I would push into my skin until the blood came.

As I think about them now I remember the sting and the white line they made; the beads of red pushing out. I remember licking the blood and tasting iron on my tongue. Dropping the pieces from the window as we drove. Watching them fly from my hand.

ABOUT THE AUTHORS

Ismail Karolia

Ismail was born in Bradford, West Yorkshire, in 1983 and has five brothers and four sisters. From the age of nine Ismail, along with his siblings, was taken into care. He stayed in the care of his elder sister, Hameeda, until his teen years. After this, he moved around a lot, living with foster carers and his sister Mariyam. Ismail remained nomadic until 2006, when he settled in Blackburn following marriage to Asma Mayat, a born and bred Blackburnian. He completed his final year of a BA (Hons) English Language and Literary studies at Blackburn College's Institute of Higher Education, having completed two years of studies at University of Central England, Birmingham. Ismail has since received a Masters degree in Developing Professional Practice in Management from Lancaster University and is currently working at West Lancashire Council for Voluntary Service. He has two children, Bilaal and Issa.

Tony O'Neill

I was born in and raised in Blackburn, and my family is still there. This poem was an attempt to reconcile some of my conflicted feelings about the town, and its place in my psyche.

Like most people, when I was younger I was eager to get out of my hometown and see the world. I suppose it is only in retrospect that I have been able to appreciate some of the things about Blackburn that I maybe didn't think about when I was younger. I've lived away from Blackburn since I was 18, but still come back whenever I can to visit family. I've written 7 books in all, novels, short stories, poetry and non-fiction. I began writing in the aftermath of a 7-plus year period of heroin addiction; I suppose it was as much a kind of therapy as anything else. That first book - a novel about my experiences as a heroin addict in Los Angeles - led to a writing career that was probably as much a surprise to me as it has been to the people around me.

John Hindle

The poem was inspired by memories of my childhood and my experience of Primary school in Blackburn. My father's side of the family is from Blackburn. I wrote the piece as a reflection of the years I spent in Blackburn and in particular the centenary year of the school. I started writing as a teenager in order to express my thoughts and feelings about life. Recently, I completed a Masters Degree in Creative writing.

David R Morgan

Author David R Morgan teaches 11-19 year olds at Cardinal Newman School in Luton, and lives in Bedfordshire with his ex -wife and two children. His eldest daughter lives in The Isle of Man.

David has been an arts worker and literature officer, organizer of book festivals and writer-in-residence for education authorities, Littlehay Prison and Fairfield Psychiatric Hospital (which was the subject of a Channel 4 film, Out of Our Minds). He has had two plays screened on ITV.

His books for children include: *The strange Case of William Whipper-Snapper*, three *Info Rider* books for Collins and *Blooming Cats.* The latter won the Acorn Award and was recently animated for BBC2's Words and Pictures Plus, as well as a Horrible Histories biography: *Spilling The Beans On Boudicca*. David has also written poetry books, including: *The Broken Picture Book*, The *Windmill and the Grains* (Hawthorn Prize) and *Buzz Off.*

His poetry collection *Walrus on a Rocking Chair*, illustrated by John Welding, is published by *Claire Publications* and his adult poetry *Ticket for the Peepshow* is published by *art'icle and Poetry Space.*

MARK ELLIS

Mark Ellis is a liar.

KEITH DALTON

Keith is divorced with three children (one lives in Australia), and plans to marry later this year. He has lived in Blackburn, off and on, since 1972 and has been writing, off and on, since his twenties. He wrote Northern Street because it appeared in front of him, which poems often do. He started writing because he felt a desire to do it. He writes poetry, odd bits of prose, mostly humour, and is also a singer songwriter, and striving manfully to finish a long novel.

A.J. ASHWORTH

A.J. Ashworth was born and brought up in Blackburn and only recently moved away. This story was inspired by childhood trips to Heysham with her family, all of whom still live in Blackburn, although the accident was fictionalised from someone else's account. A.J. won Salt Publishing's 2011 Scott Prize and her short story collection 'Somewhere Else, or Even Here' will be published by them this year. Her work has been published in a number of magazines, including The Warwick Review and Tears in the Fence, as well as being listed in competitions including the Willesden Herald International Short Story Competition, the Short Fiction Competition and Fish Short Story Prize. She has a certificate in creative writing from Lancaster University and an MA in Writing (distinction) from Sheffield Hallam. You can follow her @ajashworth

BARON JEPSON

However hard life is or gets don't give up. My name is Baron Jepson born on September 2nd 1972 at Queen's Park hospital Blackburn, into what I thought was the most wonderful life imaginable. I still feel the wonder is there, only we forget to look. Life has a funny way of dragging us along for the ride, and with all the mayhem in the world it is hard to see the beauty. I have experienced major setbacks throughout my life making it hard to stay the course; nevertheless I am still pushing forwards searching for the garden.

Amanda is my wife and guiding star, she has given me two beautiful girls who are my inspiration; they have a brother from an earlier relationship, who is an absolute credit, not only to himself, but to his mother who raised him.

The story you read is an extract of memories, from much more simplistic times, that help me to see the path, and why it all matters.

COTTON TOWN PROJECT BY THE YOUTH ACTION AMBASSADORS GROUP

This group consists of young people who aim to explore important issues that affect us. We like to learn new things as well as gain new experiences. We have engaged in a range of pioneering projects like an Interfaith Project, Healthy Living Project, Community Cohesion, Fundraising and much more. One of the projects that group members were involved in was the Cotton Town Project. This combined community cohesion, history and intergenerational communication as we brought members of all communities and different age groups to explore issues around our shared history. The group was so proud of this project that we wanted to write something to reflect on our achievement

GAYE GERRARD

Gaye was born in Crewe but now lives in Bolton where she has spent most of her life. She has an M.A. in Creative Writing and writes poetry and short stories. She is currently working on the final stages of a children's historical novel which has had the gestation period of several elephants!

Gaye writes most prolifically when moored in seclusion on the family's narrow boat in the Yorkshire Dales. Her inspiration is drawn from many sources, including experiences whilst travelling abroad. She participates in performance readings and, as a member of East Lancs Writers, based at BBC Radio Lancashire, she has enjoyed a variety of opportunities to contribute to live and recorded broadcasts.

Her work has been published in many anthologies including 'At The Kitchen Table ,' published by the BBC and incorporating the work of some of 'Lancashire's leading literary lights.' She has also published 'Behind a Door ,' an anthology of writing by residents of a women's refuge. Gaye was also Writer in Residence at Fortalice for quite a time (after this was published) and have been involved in one way or another for 30 years from being a founder member.

DIANE SMITH

Di Smith's mother was born in Blackburn in 1914. After living in the south, she eventually returned to her roots in the 1980s. Di was born in Surrey and remembers the arduous trips north in the days before the M1. She wrote the piece to capture the strangeness of Blackburn to a young child. She visits her mother regularly, but sadly her grandparents, uncle and aunts have all now died. She enjoys meeting her two cousins, who both live in Blackburn and are a great support to her mother. Di's first career was in the National Health Service, latterly moving into management consulting. She started writing for fun when she was about nine, but only took it up as a career in 2004 after gaining a journalism MA. She is currently a freelance business writer and studying for a Diploma in Creative Writing with the Open University.

THOMAS ECCLES

My name is Thomas Eccles I am 19 years old and currently studying Graphic Design at Blackburn University. I have lived in Blackburn all my life with my mum and my dad and my brother. We lived in Mill Hill for around 13 years until we moved nearer to the Witton area. I've always enjoyed writing for as long as I can remember. I currently do a lot of writing academically as well as writing a lot in other various activities, such as lyrics, poems, stories and reviews. My piece about Blackburn is just how I've always seemed to feel ever since I discovered its history, and although I don't think many people will enjoy my opinion, it's what I want to say about my hometown.

MARTIN MCAREAVEY

Martin McAreavey is a lecturer in Business and Management at the University Centre at Blackburn College, where he leads the Executive Diploma in Management Studies (EDMS) Program. Although Martin was born locally (Preston) and raised in Blackburn, he has only recently returned to East Lancashire after a career in International Business in the US and Europe. A keen amateur musician and wordsmith, the original inspiration for 'Bag Lady' came from a conversation with a homeless woman in Covent Garden, London in the late 1990s. Having returned to Blackburn in 2006, Martin was reminded about the problem of homelessness following the publication of statistics for the region in 2008. 'Bag Lady' was written as a tribute to the lost lives of many who take to the streets as a last option, following the collapse of marriages, loss of jobs and the rise of mental health problems in our society.

ALAN TAYLOR

Alan was brought up on Tyneside but has spent most of his adult life in East Lancashire. He has a science/mathematics background and only developed an interest in Poetry after he read 'The Letters of Ted Hughes edited by Christopher Read' in late 2009. This book spurred him to read poetry of all periods from Keats to Motion and he soon attempted his own compositions.

He finds that writing Poetry helps him to express his feelings on all sorts of issues. He doesn't think that his work can generally be called contemporary because he writes a lot about nature and also likes to compose historical narratives.

'The Methodist Chapel' was inspired by a watercolour painting he saw online. He can't remember its title or artist but the picture showed a scene which is typical of many northern industrial towns, including Blackburn.

SARAH HILARY

Born in the North of England, to a mother who was a child survivor of a Japanese PoW camp and a father whose family hailed from Blackburn, Sarah Hilary is the winner of the Sense Creative Writing Award 2010 and the Fish Criminally Short Histories Prize 2008. Her family moved to Bristol in 2009. Sarah writes to keep herself company, and in the hope of entertaining her readers. An award-winning short story writer, she is working on her first novel. Her agent is Jane Gregory.

SHANE MCHUGH

Shane was born in Blackburn. He is a young person who has seen the transmission of childhood to adulthood in Blackburn. This town is a great town to live but people always have their issues. Blackburn has a very large youth population and often young people are stereotypes and misunderstood by wider society. So he wanted to showcase his life as a young adult to challenge some of these views and reflect on his feelings and thoughts about being young in Blackburn.

J PALMER

'I was born into a farming family in Twiston, Lancashire, where I grew up. I went to Clitheroe Grammar School, studied German at Reading University, lived in Canterbury for a while and then taught English as a foreign language in Libya, Spain and Mexico. I lived in London for the next thirty years, teaching in various London universities. My memories of my early life were always vivid and prompted me to write 'Contrary Mary' about an episode in Blackburn Infirmary, suffering from acute bronchitis. I then turned this into an autobiographical novel called 'Nowhere better than home ,' a favourite phrase of my mother's. Nearly three years ago I returned to my birthplace to research my family history and continue writing.'

GIDEON WOODHOUSE

Born in Lancaster in 1977, I moved to Blackburn when I was two. Since then, I have lived on the Feniscowles side and vividly remember playing in the woods and fields around the area. I remember the fuss over the ice skating rink and the one house that didn't want to be removed to make way for it. After being a rep for many years travelling the highways of Britain, I am now settled once again in Blackburn and studying for the degree and career I should have done years ago.

CHRISTINE CLAYTON

Christine Clayton is a freelance music teacher, living and working in the Ormskirk area, who has written poetry, prose, stories and song-lyrics on an amateur basis since childhood. She originally became interested in Blackburn in 2008, when she began visiting the town regularly in order to trace her father's family history. Her contribution to the anthology is largely based on the experiences that led her to undertake family history studies.

LOTTE GRACIE NEIL

Lotte Gracie Neil is 11 years old. She is originally from Bedfordshire and has been living in Lancashire for the last 3 years. She loves reading, especially Phillip Pullman, Terry Pratchett, JK Rowling and Jaqueline Wilson. Lotte spends most of her own time writing and has ambitions to become an author.

MARIA ISMAIL

Maria is an English student at the University Centre Blackburn College.

PAULINE JACKSON

This is Pauline in her Tech uniform, dancing up the Mecca in school dinner break.

Printed in Great Britain
by Amazon.co.uk, Ltd.,
Marston Gate.